Let's Play

SATOMI ICHIKAWA

PHILOMEL BOOKS

First published in the United States of America
in 1981 by Philomel Books, a division of The
Putnam Publishing Group, 200 Madison Avenue,
New York, N.Y. 10016.
Copyright © 1981 by Satomi Ichikawa.
(First published in Great Britain by William
Heinemann, Ltd., 1981)
All rights reserved. Printed in Great Britain.

Library of Congress Cataloging in Publication Data

Ichikawa, Satomi.
    Let's play.

    Summary: Depicts the various things "we" can
play with, such as balloons, crayons, dolls, etc.
    [1. Play--Fiction] I. Title.
PZ7.Il6Le 1982   [E]   81-1730
ISBN 0-399-20824-0   AACR2
ISBN 0-399-61186-X (lib. bdg.)

Let's play together.
Let's play with the . . .

train

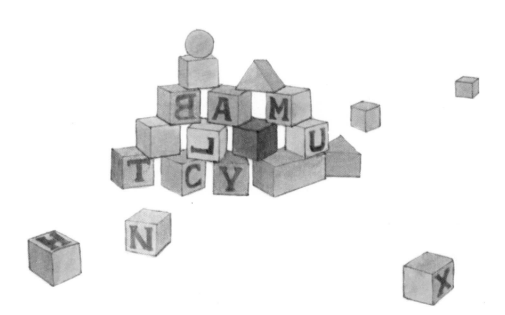

blocks

ball

dolls

tambourine

rocking horse

ball^oons

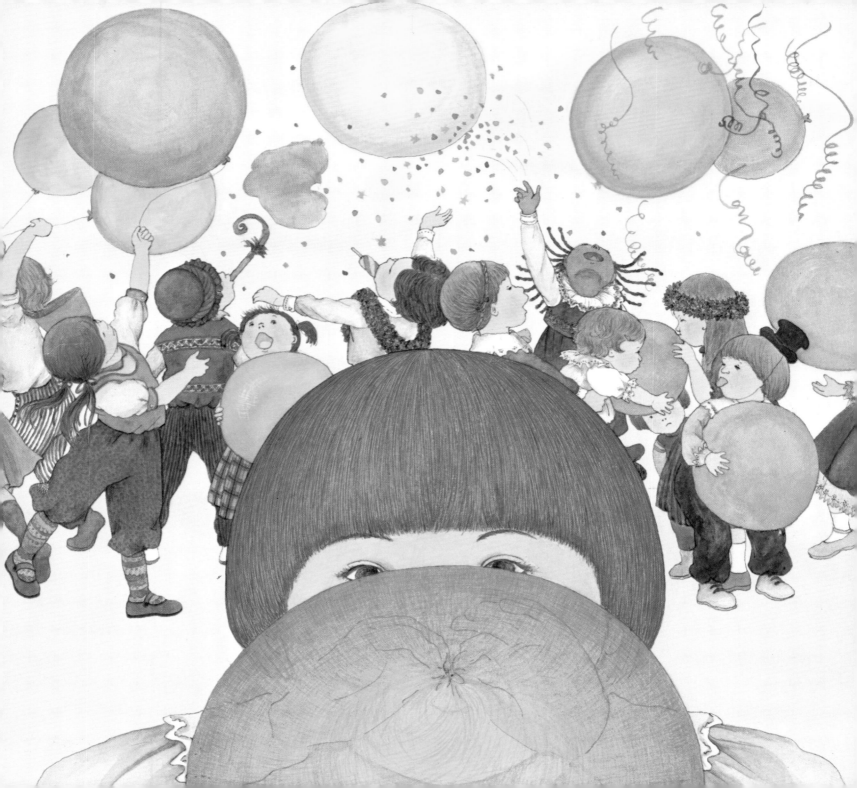

playhouse

car

dress-up clothes

pails

one rake

two shovels

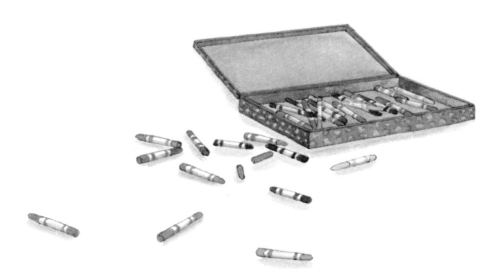

crayons

boat

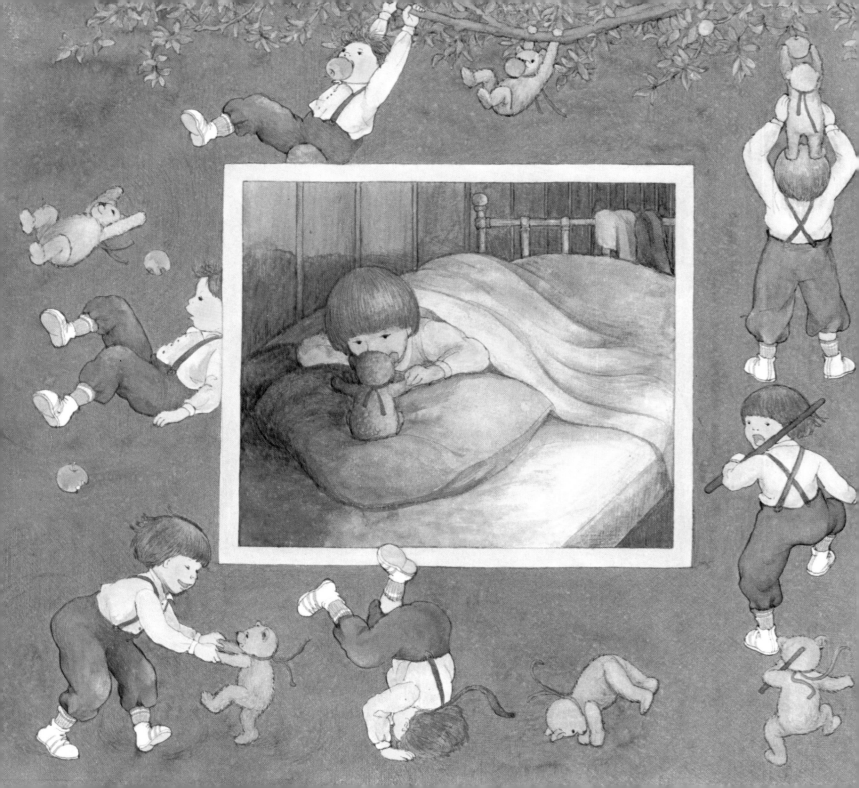

teddy bear